This book belongs to

....

Copyright © 2013

make believe ideas ltd

The Wilderness, Berkhamsted, Hertfordshire, HP4 2AZ, UK.
565 Royal Parkway, Nashville, TN 37214, USA.

www.makebelieveideas.com

Written by Tim Bugbird.
Illustrated by Stuart Lynch.
Designed by Annie Simpson and Sarah Vince.

Paulette
the pinkest puppy in the world

Tim Bugbird · Stuart Lynch

make
believe
ideas

This is the tale of a puppy –
a puppy whose name was Paulette.
She was much like her brothers and sisters,
with a difference you'd never forget.

She had blue eyes like her sister, Bessy,
and big ears like her brother, Dale,
and just like her cousin, Jessy,
the cutest curly tail.

But one quite remarkable feature
meant Paulette was never in sync.
A truly unusual creature . . .

Paulette was
totally
PINK!

Not **gold**,

not **brown**,

not **black**,

or **white**,

not **green**,

or **red**,

or **blue**,

or **purple**,

or **yellow**
(with **dots** and **stripes**),

Paulette was **too pink** to be true!

This would have been **fine** and *dandy*

for a *piglet*,

a starfish,

or bird.

But a **puppy**
the color of **candy?**
The idea was simply
absurd!

Wherever she went, puppies would point and say,

"Well, look at that!

Paulette looks silly.

I mean, really?"

So she tried to hide under a hat!

But the trouble with wearing a big, floppy hat, while it covered up some of the pink,

was she'd bump into things with a
BANG and a SPLAT!
It drove Paulette to the brink!

And then, one day, she had a FALL –
it was **truly** the **final** straw.
Her face **covered up**,
she saw **nothing** at all

and **tripped** on a **trike** to the floor!

She knocked herself out but soon came around,
and she grabbed what she thought was a post.
But the post was a ladder, not stuck in the ground.
"Uh-oh!" she thought, "I'm toast!"

As the ladder wobbled, it knocked a pail
of paint that was high on a sill.
The puppies below began to wail,
"Look out! It's going to spill!"

The petrified pups simply **froze** – they didn't have time to **think.**

Covered in gunk from their heads to their toes – their coats were sticky and pink!

The goop wouldn't wash out
and nor would the goo,
so Paulette's mom
took out her clippers.
There was only one thing
she could possibly do,
but it gave the poor pups
the shivers!

Paulette's mom clipped each one –
it felt like such a shame.

But the puppies saw,
when the job was done,
underneath they were all the same!

"You're not so different after all,"
said Mom to Paulette with a wink.

"And when they look back,
I think they'll recall
it was nice to be a bit pink!"

It could have been a **disastrous** day had Paulette not been the kind to look at things a **different** way. From the **fuss** a **thought** sprung to mind!

She opened a salon –

Pink Cutz and More –

giving pedicures, perms, and dyes.

She was the **bark** of the park,

now everyone saw

Paulette through a fresh pair of eyes.

Pink Cutz & More!

Her **clientele** were the **smartest** in town,
with coats **combed**, **braided**, and **curled**.

And Paulette became **famous** for miles around . . .

for being the **happiest pup** in the **world**!